Spider McDrew

Roaring Good Reads will fire the imagination
of all young readers – from short stories for children just
starting to read on their own, to first chapter books and
short novels for confident readers.
www.roaringgoodreads.co.uk

Also by Alan Durant

Happy Birthday, Spider McDrew
Little Troll
Little Troll and the Big Present

More Roaring Good Reads from Collins

Spider McDrew

Alan Durant

Illustrated by Philip Hopman

An imprint of HarperCollinsPublishers

This one is for Ann-Janine,
editor supreme and excellent pal.

First published in Great Britain by CollinsChildren'sBooks in 1996
This edition published in Great Britain by Collins in 2002
Collins is an imprint of HarperCollins*Publishers* Ltd
77-85 Fulham Palace Road, Hammersmith, London W6 8JB

The HarperCollins website address is www.fireandwater.com

1 3 5 7 9 8 6 4 2

Text copyright © Alan Durant
Illustrations by Philip Hopman

ISBN 0 00 767523 2

The author asserts the moral right to be
identified as the author of the work.

Printed and bound in England by Bookmarque Ltd, Croydon

Contents

Spider's Big Match

Spider McDrew was a hopeless case. Everyone said so. His mother said it each morning when Spider came down to breakfast wearing one blue sock and one orange sock, or with his jumper on back to front.

"Oh, Spider," she said, shaking her head sadly, "you're a hopeless case."

Mr Smithers, his teacher at Parkfield School, said it too, whenever he asked Spider a question and got the wrong answer.

"What's five times six, Spider?"

"Ninety-four million, sir."

"What's the capital of France, Spider?"

"The Atlantic Ocean, sir."

"Spider McDrew, you're a hopeless case."

It wasn't that Spider was stupid. He knew that five times six is thirty. He knew that the capital of France is Paris. It was just that his mind wandered and he was always one step behind everyone else. One moment he was sitting listening to Mr Smithers and then it was as if a bee came buzzing by and suddenly he was thinking about something else completely. The answers he gave were to questions that Mr Smithers had asked a long time before. How many miles is the sun from the Earth? What ocean separates Europe and America?

The children in his class thought Spider was hopeless too. He was always messing up their playground games.

"You're it, Spider," said Darren Kelly, when they were playing tag. Spider frowned. Then he took a step forward.

"What's the time, Mr Wolf?" he cried.

The other children groaned. "We're not playing that game any more, Spider," said Jason Best.

"You're hopeless, Spider," said Kip Keen.

The children didn't ask Spider to play any more. At breaktime, he just wandered round the playground, in a world of his own, daydreaming. He looked a real sight too. His clothes were a mess, his shoes were scuffed and his coal-black hair sprouted wildly from his head like the leaves of a spider plant. That's why his nickname was Spider. His real name was Spencer, but hardly anybody called him that. Even his mother called him Spider most of the time. He was Spider McDrew, the hopeless case.

Parkfield was only a small village school, but it had a very good football team. In fact, with just one match left to play, Parkfield was top of the league.

"All we need is to draw our last game against Stoneley and we'll be champions," Mr Smithers told his team. "But if Stoneley

win, then they'll be champions." It was a very important match.

"Don't worry, sir, we'll win," said Neil "Deadeye" Phillips, Parkfield's ace striker and captain.

"Yeah, we'll destroy them," snarled Darren Kelly. He punched the air and made loud, destroying noises.

"Darren," said Mr Smithers, "it's a football match, not World War Three."

Everyone was excited about the match – even girls like Emma Flowers and Hannah Stewart, who hated football.

"I'm sure we'll win – and so's Barbie," said Hannah Stewart. Barbie was Hannah Stewart's favourite toy.

"Snuggles is sure we'll win too. He says we'll win four love," said Emma Flowers. Snuggles was Emma Flowers's new pet, a golden brown and white guinea pig which she loved very much. Spider was very excited about the match too, even though he wasn't in the team.

Then, the day before the match, disaster struck. Chickenpox hit Parkfield! One by one, the football team broke out in rashes and spots: Kip Keen, Matthew Jones, Verbushan Patel, Neil Phillips... As each was sent home, Mr Smithers had to call up a reserve to take his place. But by the end of the afternoon, Mr Smithers still needed one more player.

"My brother's brilliant," Darren Kelly suggested. "He's top scorer for his school."

"That's very good, Darren," said Mr Smithers. "But we can only choose children who go to Parkfield. I think your brother's a bit old for our team, too, don't you?" Darren Kelly's brother was fourteen.

"We could play a man short," said Jason Best, who was the team captain now that Neil Phillips had chickenpox. "Teams play better with only ten men. Gary Lineker said so."

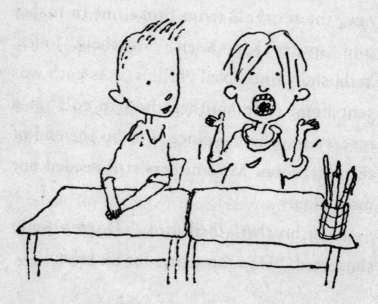

"Mmm," said Mr Smithers. "That's very interesting Jason, but I think we have to start the match with a full team." He looked round the class with a heavy heart. He had no choice: Spider would have to play.

Spider was delighted. He smiled like he'd never smiled before.

"I won't let you down, sir," he said. "I'll..." But what he would do no one ever knew, for at that moment, his mind wandered. Mr Smithers shrugged his shoulders and sighed.

On the way home, Spider happily kicked stones along the pavement. He was in the football team – *he*, Spider McDrew! He jumped and waved his arms in the air as he'd seen Neil Phillips do when he scored a goal. Then, bump, he slipped on some wet leaves and fell on his bottom. At the same time, his mind wandered from football to nature.

"I wonder if leaves have feelings?" he thought, as he picked himself up. He was very careful not to tread on any, just in case.

Spider was almost home when he saw a ball on the path in front of him. Without thinking, he kicked at it. He aimed a straight kick, but instead he kicked *across* the ball.

He watched in surprise as the ball curved away like a banana. Through the air it soared, across the road and... wham! Straight into his mother's best potted geranium!

Crash! Smash!

The flowerpot tipped over and broke on the concrete path. The front door opened and his mum appeared. She looked very angry.

"Spider!" she cried. "Whatever do you think you're doing!"

Spider was very sorry. He helped his mum pick up the pieces of broken flowerpot and tried to explain what had happened. Luckily, the geranium wasn't damaged. His mum scooped it up gently and put it into another pot.

"You really must be more careful, Spider," she said. "If you want to play football, go to the park."

"Yes, Mum," said Spider. Then he remembered about the big match.

"Mum," he said. "I'm in the football team!" Spider's mum could hardly believe her ears. She nearly dropped the new flowerpot.

"That's wonderful," she said.

Spider told his mum the whole story.

"It's lucky you've had chickenpox," she said.

"Will you come and watch me play?" Spider asked.

"I wouldn't miss it for the world," said Spider's mum. She gave Spider a kiss. "I'll leave work early. But I might not be there for the start."

"That's OK. Thanks, Mum," said Spider happily.

Spider's mum ruffled his hair so that it looked even more sprouty than usual. "I'll expect you to score a goal, of course," she said. "Spider. Spider?"

Spider looked at her blankly. He wasn't thinking about football any more.

"Mum, do leaves have feelings?" he asked. Spider's mum shook her head and smiled.

"You're a hopeless case, Spider McDrew!" she laughed.

The next afternoon, when Spider stood waiting for the kick-off, he felt very nervous. He so wanted to do well that his stomach was a-flutter with butterflies. Lots of parents had come to see the match, but Spider couldn't see his mum.

"Come on, Stoneley!" shouted the Stoneley parents.

"Come on, Parkfield!" shouted the Parkfield parents.

Mr Smithers blew his whistle. The game was on!

For most of the first half, Stoneley were on the attack. The play was all in the Parkfield half and Spider hardly got a kick. He watched as a Stoneley striker hit a terrific shot that soared towards the top corner of the net. It looked a goal all the way. But no, the Parkfield goalkeeper, Jack Smith, sprang like a cat through the air and turned the ball around the post.

"Great save!" the crowd cried.

Jason Best waved at Spider.

"Everyone back for the corner," he called.

"Come on, Spider!" shouted Darren Kelly. Spider ran back quickly.

"Stand in the goalmouth by that post, Spider," Jason ordered.

The corner came over. The Stoneley striker rose highest and headed the ball. It looped across the goal, over the hands of

Jack Smith, towards Spider on the goal line.

"Get it away, Spider!" his team-mates shouted. But Spider was still thinking about Jack Smith's brilliant save and instead of heading the ball he dived and pushed it round the post with his hand.

"Penalty!"

Mr Smithers blew his whistle and pointed to the penalty spot.

The Stoneley striker stepped forward and wham, the ball flew into the Parkfield net! Stoneley were in the lead! The Stoneley players and supporters jumped for joy. The Parkfield players and supporters groaned.

Spider hung his head in shame. He'd let the whole school down. He was glad his mum hadn't arrived. When the half-time whistle blew, he just wanted to run away and hide. But

Mr Smithers called the whole team around him and gave them a stern talking to.

"You're giving the ball away too much," he said. "You've got to think more and try harder."

Spider waited for his teacher to tell him he was a hopeless case for what he'd done. But Mr Smithers didn't say anything about the penalty. As the players lined up for the second-half kick-off, he put his hand on Spider's shoulder. "Don't let your head drop, lad," he said quietly. "Just do your best."

These few, kind words had a big effect on Spider. He went out for the second half with new heart and determination.

Straight from the kick-off, Parkfield went on the attack. They passed the ball around carefully, waiting for an opening. Spider played his part, running hard and not giving the ball away once. Parkfield got a corner and another one... They had lots of shots. They hit the bar and the post. But still a goal would not come. Then, with ten minutes left, Jason Best burst through the Stoneley defence and, as the goalkeeper came out, he chipped the ball beautifully... just over the bar.

"Great try!" shouted the Parkfield crowd.

The next time Spider got the ball, he kept it instead of passing. He turned past one defender, nutmegged a second, pushing the ball between his legs, and skipped over the tackle of a third.

The Parkfield crowd bayed with excitement, as Spider swerved past the last defender and sent the Stoneley goalkeeper tumbling into the mud.

The goal was at Spider's mercy. No one could catch him.

"Shoot!" cried the crowd.

With great care, Spider drew back his foot... and chipped the ball just over the bar, exactly as his captain had done.

For a moment there was a shocked silence. The players of both sides stood stock-still, boggle-eyed. The crowd lost its voice. Mr Smithers, who had been about to blow for a goal, nearly swallowed his whistle.

Then everyone started to shout at once. Darren Kelly yelped and threw himself backwards into the mud. Jason Best rushed up to Spider and pushed his finger into his chest.

"You useless idiot, Spider," he said. "What were you thinking of?"

"I was trying to do what you did," Spider said unhappily. "I'm sorry."

"Sorry?" said his captain fiercely. "You've just lost us the championship." He sent Spider off to the wing, where he'd be out of the way.

The game was almost over. Standing out

near the touchline, all by himself, Spider was a pitiful sight. He was muddy from head to toe, his shirt hung out of his shorts, his socks drooped round his ankles, his black hair was a spiky mess. He looked like he was about to burst into tears.

Parkfield mounted one last attack. Zoe Cole ran into the penalty area and shot; the Stoneley goalkeeper pushed the ball round the post.

"Corner kick," said Mr Smithers. He kicked the ball out towards Spider.

"Take it, Spider," Jason Best shouted.

"Hurry up, Spider," called Darren Kelly.

Spider stumbled over to the corner flag. But as he stepped back to take the kick, his mind wandered. It wandered so far that his whole head felt empty.

Mr Smithers blew his whistle. The crowd shouted. His team-mates waved and shrieked. But Spider looked as if he had turned to stone.

Then he caught sight of someone in the crowd. It was his mum! Her face was bright red and she was puffing. She waved to Spider.

In an instant, Spider's mind slid back into place.

"Swing it in, Spider!" Jason Best screamed.

Spider recalled the afternoon before and that amazing banana kick. He saw in his mind the ball hitting that flowerpot... With a spring, he ran forward and kicked across the ball with the top of his right foot.

The ball soared across the pitch towards the Stoneley penalty area. The Parkfield crowd groaned as the ball went away from the Stoneley goal.

But then it happened! The ball started to swerve. It curved back in towards the Stoneley goal. The crowd roared. Too late, the Stoneley goalkeeper saw the danger and threw himself to his left. But the dipping ball passed his fingertips and flew into the net.

"Goal!"

Spider had scored!

The Parkfield crowd went wild. No one heard Mr Smithers blow his whistle for the end of the match. Parkfield had equalized with the very last kick. It was a draw and Parkfield, not Stoneley, were champions.

The Parkfield players were over the moon. They jumped in the air, they shouted, they danced and hugged each other. Then they lifted Spider up on their shoulders and carried him off the field.

"Well done, Spider," said Mr Smithers. "Well done! I knew you could do it." Then he turned to Spider's mum.

"That boy's got great potential, Mrs McDrew," he said.

Spider's mum beamed. Then she planted a big kiss on Spider's muddy forehead.

"I got here just in time," she said. "You are clever, Spider."

Spider looked puzzled.

"Did we win then?" he asked.

Spider's Special Pet

Parkfield School needed money to build a nature garden. Mrs Merridew, the head teacher, had just told everyone about it in assembly. She said that the school was going to have a fund-raising week and she wanted every class to help by doing an event.

"It doesn't have to be anything big," she said. "Every little counts."

"Now, I wonder," said Mr Smithers, when his class were back in their room again, "has anyone got any good ideas?" Darren Kelly, as usual, was the first to put up his hand.

"Please, sir," he said. "Why don't we buy loads of sweets and sell them?" Darren Kelly loved sweets.

"Sweets aren't allowed at school," piped Hannah Stewart.

"No, that's right, Hannah," Mr Smithers agreed.

Jason Best's hand went up.

"We could have a sponsored swim," he said. Jason Best loved swimming. It was his second favourite thing, after football.

"Yeah great," said Kip Keen. "I like swimming." He thrashed his hands about in front of him, whacking Emma Flowers on the head.

"Ow!" she squealed.

"Thank you, Kip, that will do," said Mr Smithers.

"I can't swim," said Hannah Stewart.

"I can't either," said Jack Smith.

"Well, anyway," said Mr Smithers, "we don't have a swimming pool, so a sponsored swim is out. Still, it was a good idea, Jason." Jason Best smiled and looked very pleased with himself.

"Anyone else?" Mr Smithers prompted.

"What about a pet show?" said Emma Flowers. "It could be a competition and we could all pay some money to enter." Emma Flowers thought her guinea pig, Snuggles, was the best and most beautiful pet in the world.

"Mmm, that's a good idea, Emma," said Mr Smithers.

Darren Kelly's hand shot up. "Please sir, I've got a rat and a gerbil and a dog," he said breathlessly. "I used to have two rats but my dog ate one."

"My cat ate my brother's hamster," said Hannah Stewart.

Suddenly everyone started talking about their pets and the things they had done. Mr Smithers clapped his hands.

"OK," he said, "that will do." A picture came into his head of dogs chasing cats and cats pouncing on hamsters and goldfish vanishing from their bowls – of mess and tears and terrible noise... No, a pet show was not such a good idea, he decided. "I'm afraid Mrs Merridew doesn't allow pets in school," he said.

There was a groan of disappointment.

Spider McDrew put up his hand.

"Ah, Spider's got an idea," said Mr Smithers. "Let's hear it then, Spider."

Everyone turned to look at Spider, who gave a little cough.

"We could all bring a bucket," he said with a hopeful smile.

There was a moment of total silence. Then Jason Best said, "What's he talking about, sir? I don't want to bring a bucket."

"I'm sure Spider will explain, won't you Spider?" Mr Smithers said gently.

"We could all bring a bucket of water to make a swimming pool," Spider explained proudly.

The class groaned again.

"Spider," said Mr Smithers. "We're not doing a sponsored swim. We've already decided that. We're not doing a pet show either."

"Oh," said Spider and his face fell. Even his spiky hair seemed to droop.

"Try to pay attention, Spider," Mr Smithers said. Then he turned to the rest of the class. "Any more ideas?" he asked. This time no hands went up.

"Mmm," said Mr Smithers. "Well, I have an idea. What about a special Show and Tell?" Show and Tell was something that the class did every week. They brought in things which they showed to the rest of the class, saying why they liked them. Often the things were for the nature table – conkers or prickly horse-chestnut shells or brightly-coloured leaves. Toys though, were not allowed.

"Why will it be special?" asked Emma Flowers.

"Because for this Show and Tell you can bring in your favourite thing – and that includes toys," said Mr Smithers with a smile.

Everyone was very enthusiastic about this suggestion. It was agreed that for fifty pence anyone could bring in his or her favourite thing to show the rest of the class.

The children were still chattering about the special Show and Tell when they left school later that afternoon – all except Spider. He was thinking about pets – and in particular, his own pet. Spider's pet was not a cat or a dog or a rabbit or a hamster or a guinea pig or a mouse. It was a cow called Molly. She really belonged to Spider's gran, who had been a farmer. But Gran had moved into an old people's home and now Spider and his mum looked after Molly. She lived in a field at the back of their house which belonged to one of Gran's farmer friends.

When he wasn't at school or helping his mum around the house, Spider spent most of his time in the field with Molly. He could sit on the fence and think and dream or say whatever came into his head. Molly was a very good listener. She never got cross with him or called him a hopeless case. She just stood, or lay, swishing her tail and chewing, staring at Spider with her big, beautiful brown eyes. Spider adored her.

"Hi, Molly," Spider called when he

reached her field that afternoon. Then he watched as she lumbered slowly across the field towards him, just as she always did.

He stroked along the soft streak of white that ran down her head to her nose and she lowed gently. Then he sat down on the fence and told her all about the fund-raising week and about the sponsored swim and about the pet show. He didn't mention the Show and Tell though, because that idea had slipped out of his head. He sat happily, talking, and daydreaming with Molly, until he heard his mother calling him in for tea.

"So, Spider," she said, when he came in. "What great event is your class planning?" She was holding one of Mrs Merridew's newsletters. Spider looked at her blankly for a moment, then he said, "A pet show."

"A pet show?" His mum laughed. "That sounds like a recipe for disaster if ever I heard one." At that moment the 'phone rang. It was Jack Smith's mum asking if Spider had Jack's lunch box because she had Spider's. Spider's mum checked.

"Yes," she sighed, "he's got it."

Spider's mum went on talking for a bit. When she put down the receiver, she looked at Spider and rolled her eyes.

"Spider McDrew," she said, "you are a hopeless case. It's not a pet show you're doing, it's a special Show and Tell!"

"Oh," said Spider. He frowned, as another completely different subject entered his head. "How many buckets of water do you think you'd need to make a swimming pool?" he asked.

At last, the fund-raising week arrived. The whole school was busy with events. One class was doing a can recycling collection, another was doing a sponsored read, a third was baking cakes and biscuits to sell. All the children in Spider's class wanted to do the special Show and Tell, so Mr Smithers split them into five groups, one for each day of the week. Spider's turn was on Thursday.

The first to show and tell on Monday morning was Matthew Jones. He came to the front of the class and gave Mr Smithers his fifty pence. Then he opened a plastic carrier bag and, very carefully, took out a model of a famous ship called the *Cutty Sark*.

"I made it with my dad," he said, and he told the class all about the ship. Darren Kelly and Kip Keen wanted to know how many guns the ship had and how many battles it had fought.

"Battles are stupid," said Hannah Stewart and some of the other girls agreed – which very nearly started a battle right there in the classroom. So Mr Smithers quickly called up Hannah to show and tell. She showed her Barbie doll with lots of different sets of clothes. Her favourite, she said, was

the wedding dress. Kip Keen said it looked like a ghost costume. Hannah Stewart said Kip Keen looked like a hairy monkey.

"OK, Hannah, that will do," said Mr Smithers. Then he asked Luxmie to come up and show what she had brought.

Spider didn't know what to bring in. Monday passed, then Tuesday. Wednesday came and he still couldn't decide. He didn't have a favourite toy. He could bring in the football his mother had given him, but it was rather flat and dirty.

"What about the watch Granny gave you?" his mother suggested. Spider looked at the watch on his wrist. The time, it said, was half past two. It had been half past two for several weeks.

"It's stopped," he said.

"Oh Spider," said his mum. "Why didn't you tell me? I'd have bought you a new battery."

Spider frowned for a moment and then his face lit up in a brilliant smile. "I could pump it up," he said.

"What?" said his mum. "Pump up a watch!"

"No, my football," said Spider.

"Spider McDrew," his mum sighed, "you really are a hopeless case."

"Anyway," she added, "we haven't got a pump."

When Spider went to bed that night, he was no closer to knowing what to show and tell. But as soon as his eyes opened the next morning, he suddenly saw the answer. He would take the photograph of Molly that stood on the table by his bed. After all, there was nothing he loved more than Molly, apart from his mum and his gran. He would show the photo and tell the class all about his special pet – his cow. He set off for school feeling very excited.

Spider had to wait until last for his turn. He watched Neil Phillips send his radio-controlled car zooming and weaving round the room, until it crashed into a cupboard.

Then Darren Kelly made a lot of noise, shooting everyone with his space zapper gun, and Emma Flowers brought "ooohs" of wonder from both girls and boys with her amazing glow-stones that shone when you clicked them together.

Jason Best was the last to go before Spider. He brought in two things. He had a cup that he had won at a swimming gala and a signed poster of the Manchester United football team.

"That's not fair, sir," Hannah Stewart complained. "You said one thing. I could've brought in my scary dinosaur toy, as well as my Barbie."

"But they're both my favourite things," said Jason Best.

"No Jason," said Mr Smithers, "Hannah's right. You must choose one thing." So Jason chose the football picture. This started a heated discussion among the boys about which football team was the best and why all the others were useless and couldn't score a goal for toffee. In the end

Mr Smithers had to blow his football whistle to make everyone quiet again.

"Right," he said. "Let's have some hush. Spider's got something to show us."

Spider picked up his photograph and walked to the front of the class. His hand shook a little as he put his fifty pence in the box. Mr Smithers gave him a nod of encouragement and he turned to face the others. Then, with a beaming smile, he held up the photograph.

The class erupted. Some of the children groaned, others giggled, some did both.

"It's a cow," said Neil Phillips in disbelief.

"Bor-ing," yawned Kip Keen.

"I think she's nice," said Emma Flowers.

"Why've you brought a picture of a cow, Spider?" called Darren Kelly.

"Well, if you'll all just be quiet," said Mr Smithers sternly, "I'm sure Spider is going to tell us."

There was silence again. All eyes were on

Spider. His voice shook a little as he said, quietly, "She's my cow."

There were more groans. "You haven't got a cow," said Jason Best.

"No," said Spider, who wanted to explain that Molly actually belonged to his gran. But the words came out wrong. Instead of saying, "She's my gran's," he said, "She's my gran."

Once again, there was uproar in the classroom.

"Spider's gran's a cow," screamed Kip Keen.

"Moooo!" went Jason Best, and Neil Phillips and Darren Kelly joined in. In an instant, the room rang with loud mooing and laughter. Mr Smithers clapped his hands.

"This is a classroom, not a farmyard!" he cried. "You're all being very rude this morning. I don't know what's got into you. Now, I don't want to hear another sound, while Spider tells us about his cow." He waited until there was total silence and then he turned to Spider. "Carry on, Spider," he said kindly. "We're all listening."

But it was no good. Spider couldn't go on. There was so much he wanted to say, but his mind had gone all fuzzy, like a TV that's had its aerial unplugged. He stood with his mouth open, his tongue sort of frozen. Seconds passed, a minute...

"Well, perhaps you could tell us about your cow another time," said Mr Smithers gently.

Sadly, Spider took his picture and went

back to his seat. There was a big lump in his throat and a burning feeling in his eyes. He'd been waiting for this moment ever since he'd woken up and now he'd ruined it.

That afternoon, Spider was even more in a dream than usual.

"Whatever's the matter?" his mum asked when he got home. "You look really down in the dumps." Spider told her what had happened.

"Oh, you poor love," she said and she ruffled his spiky hair. She made him his favourite tea – eggs and chips and spaghetti shapes – but Spider was still sad when he lay in bed that night, looking at the photograph of Molly.

The next morning, Spider left home early to see Molly before going to school. He put his nose against hers and gazed into her dark eyes.

"I'm sorry Molly," he said. She shook her large head and mooed softly, as if she were saying that it was OK, it really didn't matter. Spider kissed her on the nose.

"I love you, Molly," he said. "But I've got to go to school now. I wish you could come too."

No sooner had he said this than he started to imagine what it would be like if Molly *did* come to school. After all, *she* really was his favourite thing, not the photograph of her. He lifted the latch and opened the gate.

"Come on, Molly," he said. "You're coming to school!"

Imagine the surprise when, just a few minutes later, Spider led Molly into the crowded playground of Parkfield School. Everybody stopped what they were doing and stared. The parents looked shocked and the children laughed and lots of the younger ones rushed up to Spider and Molly.

Then Mrs Merridew appeared. She peered at Spider with his wild hair and his back-to-front jumper and she peered at the large cow, chewing lazily beside him.

"What is the meaning of this, Spencer?"

she demanded. Spider smiled. For once, his mind stayed firmly in place.

"Molly's my cow," he said. "I've brought her to Show and Tell. I brought a photo but it wasn't right."

"Spencer McDrew," said Mrs Merridew severely, "you cannot bring a cow to school, no matter what the reason." Spider's smile

drooped. He looked down at his muddy shoes.

"Now," said Mrs Merridew, "we'd better see about contacting someone to get this cow returned to its proper place..."

Mrs Merridew had only taken a couple of steps towards the school when she was stopped by a group of parents. They were smiling.

"What a lovely idea, Mrs Merridew, bringing a cow to school to show the children," said one.

"Yes," said another. "I think it's an excellent way to raise funds."

"Where do we put our money?" asked a third.

"You are collecting money, aren't you?" said a fourth.

"Well, I— er..." Mrs Merridew stuttered.

At that moment Mr Smithers appeared, carrying a bucket. "Here you are, Spider," he said, giving Spider the bucket. "Why don't you walk round the playground with Molly and then if anyone wants to give some money for the nature garden, they can put it in that."

For an instant, Spider did not move at all.

He stared open-mouthed at Mr Smithers and Mrs Merridew. Then, suddenly, his mouth shut and his eyes shone and his drooping mouth curved up again. Everything was going to be OK after all!

"Come on, Molly," he said happily.

Spider collected twelve pounds and twenty-eight pence for the nature garden. Everyone wanted to see Molly and touch her and ask Spider questions. No one groaned or giggled.

"Can you milk her?" asked Jack Smith.

"No," said Spider. "She's too old. There's no milk in her udders now."

"My mum's got udders," said Darren Kelly.

"No, she hasn't," said Hannah Stewart. "People don't have udders."

"Well, she's got milk," Darren Kelly insisted. "I've seen it."

Mr Smithers explained to Darren that his mother had milk in her breasts because she had just had a baby.

"It's the same with cows," he said. "They produce milk when they have calves. Isn't that right, Spider?" Spider nodded and smiled.

It was a very different-looking Spider who returned home that afternoon. Spider's mum saw the change at once. Spider still looked as messy as ever, but all the sadness had gone from his face. Now he looked as happy as if the next day were Christmas.

"Spider," said his mum. "Whatever has

happened?" Excitedly Spider told his mum the whole story.

"No wonder you look so pleased," said his mum. She beamed warmly at Spider. "But next time, you must ask me first, before you take Molly to  school. OK? Spider?" But Spider's mind had wandered.

"Mum," he said, "did you have milk in your breasts when I was a baby?"

Spider's mum laughed. "What a question!" she said. "Of course I did. That's why you grew up to be so big and strong."

Spider frowned. "I thought I was a hopeless case," he said.

"You're a case all right, Spider McDrew,"
said his mum. "But I wouldn't have you any
other way."

Then she gave Spider an enormous hug.

Spider and the Christmas Play

Spider was looking out of the classroom window. He was thinking about birds. Earlier that morning, Mr Smithers had asked the class what their favourite birds were.

Hannah Stewart had said a robin and Jason Best had said a golden eagle. Darren Kelly had said a pterodactyl, but Mr Smithers told him that a pterodactyl wasn't a bird, it was a winged reptile...

"Spider! Spider McDrew!"

Spider stopped looking out of the window and turned to face his teacher. Mr Smithers was shaking his head.

"A heron," Spider said. "That's my favourite."

Mr Smithers sighed.

"Spider," he said, "we're not talking about birds any more. The nature lesson is over. Mrs Russell is here. She's come to tell us about the Christmas play."

"Oh," said Spider.

Mrs Russell took Spider's class for singing and played the piano in Assembly. She had long black hair and always wore very bright clothes. When she played the piano her head wobbled as if it were on a spring. It was wobbling now as she said, "Children. Can I have your attention please." She clapped her hands together. "This year the infants will be doing their nativity play, as usual, and we are going to do the story of *The Good Little Christmas Tree.*" She smiled at the class. "Do any of you know the story of *The Good Little Christmas Tree?*"

"Is it about a Christmas tree that's never naughty?" said Hannah Stewart.

"Well, yes," said Mrs Russell.

"Is it about a Christmas tree that goes round saving people?" said Jack Smith. "Like Batman?"

"Well, not exactly," said Mrs Russell.

"We had a Christmas tree last year, miss," said Darren Kelly. "But it weren't little, it were huge."

"*Was* huge," Mrs Russell corrected him. "Was huge, Darren."

"Yes miss, it were," said Darren Kelly. "It were *really* huge."

"That's very interesting, Darren," said Mrs Russell, "but I was asking about *The Good Little Christmas Tree*. Now, listen carefully and I'll tell you the story."

Mrs Russell told the class that a father brought home the Good Little Christmas Tree as a surprise for his children. The family was very poor and this was the only present the children would get. The Tree was sad because it only had a few biscuits on its branches and it wished it could look better for the children. So it went out into the snow to see what it could find.

The Tree met some goblins and some wolves and a fisher-boy and a pedlar and some baby angels. Each of them gave the

Tree something for its branches, but it had to
give them its needles in return. In the end
it was all bare and brown like a broom.

But then St Nicholas came along and took
pity on the Tree and gave it green needles
again. Now it looked beautiful and twinkly
with candles and icicles and diamonds, and

it was very happy. The children were happy too when they saw it.

"Well, children," said Mrs Russell. "Did you like that story?"

There was a loud "Yes" from everyone – even Spider McDrew. He had listened to the whole story and his mind had not wandered once.

"Well," said Mrs Russell, "now I am going to tell you who is going to have which part in the play – and don't worry, there's a part for everyone."

Spider already knew which part he wanted. He wanted to be that Good Little Christmas Tree. He wasn't the only one. Half the class wanted to be the Tree, because it was the star part in the play. Spider didn't care about that, he just wanted to be the Tree because he liked it so much.

"Now, listen carefully," said Mrs Russell. She looked down at the piece of paper she was holding in her hand. "I'll start with the Good Little Christmas Tree." All the class were very, very quiet. Spider's heart was beating like a drum.

"Neil Phillips," Mrs Russell said. Spider sighed. Some of the other children groaned.

"Now, now, children," said Mrs Russell. "There are lots of other nice parts, you know."

The teacher looked down at her list again. "Goblins," she said. "We need three goblins."

"Not me, miss," said Emma Flowers. "Goblins are horrible."

"Not all goblins," said Mrs Russell. "Some are nice."

Darren Kelly put up his hand. "Can I be a horrible goblin, miss?" he asked. But Mrs Russell shook her head.

"The goblins are Matthew, Dylan and Luxmie. Now, for the wolves."

Darren Kelly's hand shot up again.

"Please, miss, can I be a wolf?" he begged and he roared fiercely.

"Just wait, Darren," said Mrs Russell.

She read out the names of the three wolves. "Jason, Kip and Spider... Spider?"

Spider was not listening to Mrs Russell. He was still thinking about the Good Little Christmas Tree, walking about in the snow. Jack Smith nudged him with his elbow.

"Spider!" he said. "You're a wolf."

Spider looked puzzled.

"A wolf?" he said.

"That's right, Spider," said Mrs Russell. "You and Jason and Kip are wolves."

Jason and Kip started to snarl and wave their hands like claws. Then Kip let out a blood-curdling howl and pretended to sink his teeth into Hannah Stewart, who screamed.

Mrs Russell clapped her hands. "All right, that's quite enough of that, thank you Kip," she said, wobbling her head. "Save your howling for the play." Then she carried on reading out the parts. She finished with the snowflakes, who were to start the play off with a snow dance.

"We'll begin rehearsals tomorrow," Mrs Russell told them all. Then the bell went and it was time to go home.

As usual, Spider was the last to leave. He walked home alone, thinking about the play. He didn't mind too much being a wolf, he decided. He quite liked wolves, ever since Mr Smithers had told the class that in many places they were almost extinct. He'd rather have been the Good Little Christmas Tree, but a wolf was OK. The trouble was that

Spider was not very good at being a wolf, as everyone soon discovered. He was supposed to be fierce and howl terribly. Jason Best and Kip Keen howled so terribly that Mrs Russell had to tell them, several times, to calm down a little. Mrs Merridew, the head teacher, came in once and asked if there was a tomcat locked up in a cupboard somewhere. If so, she said, could someone please let it out.

Spider's howling sounded more like a little kitten.

"Come along, Spencer," said Mrs Russell. "Think wild, fierce and hungry. Imagine you haven't eaten for a week."

"Yes, Mrs Russell," said Spider, and he did try. He even practised at home in front of the mirror, growling and snarling and waving his hands around. Once his mother caught him.

"Whatever are you doing, Spider?" she said.

"I'm practising being a wild, fierce, hungry wolf, who hasn't eaten for a week," Spider said and he howled at himself in the mirror. His mother laughed.

"It sounds like you've eaten too much and got tummy ache," she said. She looked at Spider's black, sticky-up hair and his messy clothes. "You certainly look wild though," she said.

Spider also practised the one line he had in the play. It was, "Twenty green needles." He said it to himself, over and over, at home and on the way to school and he said it perfectly. But in rehearsal he could never get it right.

"What will you take for one of your lovely red toadstools?" asked the Good Little Christmas Tree.

Spider forgot to say "Twenty green needles". Instead he said, "Oh, you can have one for free." Or else he said, "When you pluck a toadstool a bell rings in the Wolves' Den," which was what Kip Keen had just said a moment before. More often than not, though, Spider said nothing at all and the play came to a stop.

The problem was that Spider's mind kept wandering from his own part to the Good Little Christmas Tree's. He could say all of the Tree's lines – and most of the rest of the lines in the play too. But he could not say the three simple words that were his own.

The other wolves started to grumble – and so did the Good Little Christmas Tree.

"You're useless, Spider," they groaned one day, a week before the play was to be put on. "You're ruining the play."

"Now now, children," said Mrs Russell firmly. But she looked worried.

"Miss, miss, let me be the wolf!" cried a snowflake. It was Darren Kelly. "I can do it. Listen, TWENTY GREEN NEEDLES!" He said this so loudly that Emma Flowers squealed and fell off her chair.

"Thank you Darren," said Mrs Russell. "But that is not necessary." She frowned at Spider, who was looking very sorry for himself.

"I know," said the teacher suddenly. "The

wolves will all say Spider's line together."

So that is what happened. Poor Spider's one and only line had gone.

At last it was the day of the Christmas Play. Everyone was very busy. Spider's class spent the morning finishing their star display to put on the wall behind the stage.

"The stars will shine and twinkle when the lights are on," Mrs Russell said. Then she and Mr Smithers checked all the children's costumes to make sure there was nothing missing.

Spider's costume was a wolf mask he had made in class, a black jumper and a pair of black trousers with a tail sewn on. His mother had put the costume in a plastic bag to take to school. But when he left home that

morning, Spider had forgotten it. His mother
had had to run after him with it.

"Spider McDrew," she'd sighed. "You are
a hopeless case. You'd forget your head if it
wasn't attached to your body." Then she'd
kissed him and wished him good luck. "I'll

see you later on stage," she'd said. "And don't worry, everything will be fine."

But everything was not fine. At lunchtime, just half an hour before the play was due to start, something awful happened. Neil Phillips fell over in the playground and hurt his arm.

"It looks like he's broken his collar bone," Mr Smithers told Mrs Russell glumly. "He'll have to go to hospital for an x-ray."

"But what about the play?" cried Mrs Russell. Her face was very pale.

"Well, perhaps someone could read the part of the Good Little Christmas Tree," Mr Smithers suggested.

Mrs Russell shook her head. "Oh no," she said, "that just wouldn't be the same."

"What else can we do?" said Mr

Smithers. "We can't cancel the play."

The children were all very quiet. They looked at Mrs Russell. She looked as if she might cry.

Then something very strange happened. At the back of the room, a small voice started speaking the lines of the Good Little Christmas Tree. Everyone turned to stare.

oh, I wish I looked more beautiful

"Spider! Spider McDrew," called Mrs Russell. "Do you know all the Christmas Tree's lines?"

Spider looked at the teacher blankly.

"He does, miss," piped Darren Kelly. "Honest he does. I've heard him."

"Is that true, Spider?" asked Mr Smithers. Spider nodded.

Mrs Russell beamed.

"Wonderful!" she cried. "We have a Good Little Christmas Tree. Spider will play the part. The play is saved!"

The snowflakes began the play with a dance. They whirled round and round. One of them, Vabushan, got too excited. He whirled round so fast that he kept bumping into all the others. In the end the Snowflake Queen,

Hannah Stewart, gave him an angry prod in the chest. After that he calmed down and the dance went very well. The parents all clapped loudly.

Now it was Spider's turn to come on stage. He looked round at all those faces staring at him and he felt a bit shy. He hoped no one could see his legs trembling under his leafy green costume. When he spoke his first line, his voice came out all croaky and he had to stop and cough and then start again. This time the words came out fine.

"Oh," he sighed. "I wish I looked more beautiful."

He had no trouble remembering the Tree's lines, because he felt like he was the Good Little Christmas Tree, not just playing a part. But there was one tricky moment. It came in the scene with the wolves. When the wolves growled, "Twenty green needles", Spider's mind wandered. For a moment, he thought he was still a wolf and he said "Twenty green needles" too!

There was a brief, awkward silence. The wolves looked at Spider. Spider looked at the wolves.

"Say, 'no'," Jason Best hissed. He nudged Spider's arm and one of the diamonds that the goblins had just given Spider fell off onto the stage. Suddenly Spider's mind slipped back into place. He was the Good Little Christmas Tree again.

"No, no!" he cried. "You cannot have my needles."

The rest of the play went without a hitch. Spider didn't mess up a single word. He did everything right. So did all the others. At the end, the parents clapped and cheered. The children all held hands, with Spider in the middle. Then they stepped forward and took a bow.

Mrs Russell got up from the piano and came to the front of the stage. She held up her hands.

"Well, ladies and gentlemen, I hope you've all enjoyed our show," she said with a little wobble and a great big smile. "The children have all worked very hard, as I'm sure you can see. But I must mention one child in particular. That is Spencer – Spider – McDrew, who stepped in today at the very last minute and I think you'll all agree he did very, very well."

She moved to the side of the stage and gave Spider a clap and all the parents and children joined in.

And then Spider saw his mum. She was standing up and waving.

"Well done, Spider!" she called proudly.

Spider beamed. Then he waved his hands in front of him and howled like a wolf. It was the best howl he had ever done.

At the back of the stage, Mrs Merridew frowned. "I really must do something about that tomcat," she said. Then she, too, raised her hands to applaud Spider McDrew, the star of the show.

Witch's the Tears

Jenny Nimmo

Illustrated by Thierry Elfezzani

In freezing hail and howling wind, a stranger is given shelter at Theo's house – a stranger who loves telling stories and whose name is Mrs Scarum. Theo is convinced she's a witch and wishes his father would return home from his travels. But the blizzard continues and the night is long... there may be tears before morning.

ISBN 0 00 714162 9

ROARING GOOD READS

Collins

■ *An imprint of HarperCollinsPublishers*

www.roaringgoodreads.co.uk

★ MICHAEL
MORPURGO

ILLUSTRATED BY GRIFF

When Jackie finds a broken garden gnome in a
rubbish skip, she is determined to make him as good
as new. In return, Mister Skip makes Jackie's wishes
come true... almost! A fairy-tale for today from a
master storyteller.

ISBN 0 00 713474 6

An imprint of HarperCollinsPublishers

www.roaringgoodreads.co.uk

Order Form

To order direct from the publishers, just make a list of the titles you want and fill in the form below:

Name ....

Address ....

....

....

Send to: Dept 6, HarperCollins Publishers Ltd, Westerhill Road, Bishopbriggs, Glasgow G64 2QT.

Please enclose a cheque or postal order to the value of the cover price, plus:

UK & BFPO: Add £1.00 for the first book, and 25p per copy for each additional book ordered.

Overseas and Eire: Add £2.95 service charge. Books will be sent by surface mail but quotes for airmail despatch will be given on request.

A 24-hour telephone ordering service is available to holders of Visa, MasterCard, Amex or Switch cards on 0141- 772 2281.

■ *An imprint of* HarperCollins*Publishers*